Just Desserts

Created by
Mark Mayerson

Adapted by
Paul Kropp

Graphics by Studio 345

an Imprint of Stewart House Publishing Inc.

Tracy liked to do magic.

Sometimes the magic worked.

Sometimes the magic did not work.

One day Tracy tried some new magic.

It zoomed past her brother Warren.

Zap! The magic hit mom and dad.

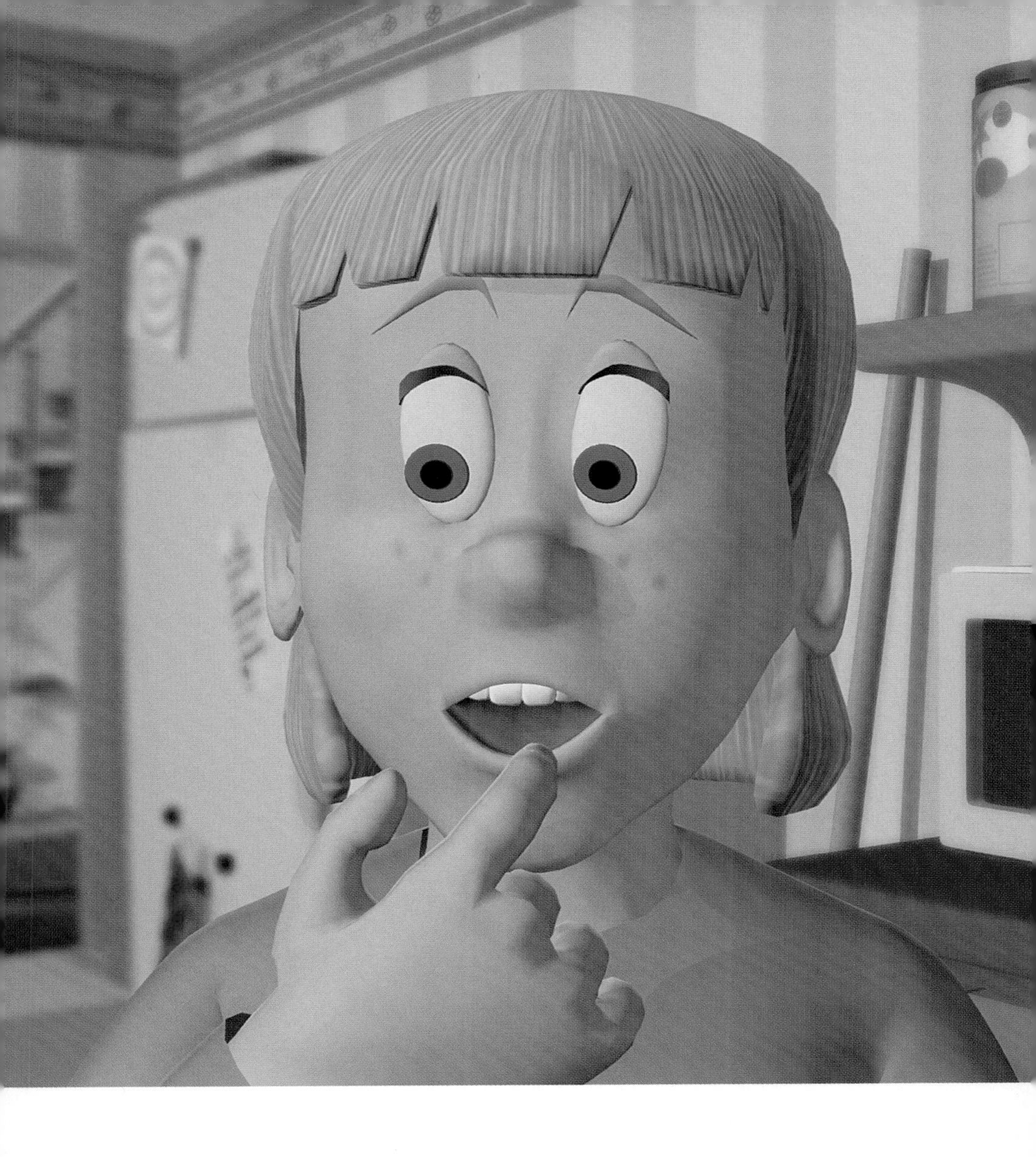

"Oh no!" Tracy cried.

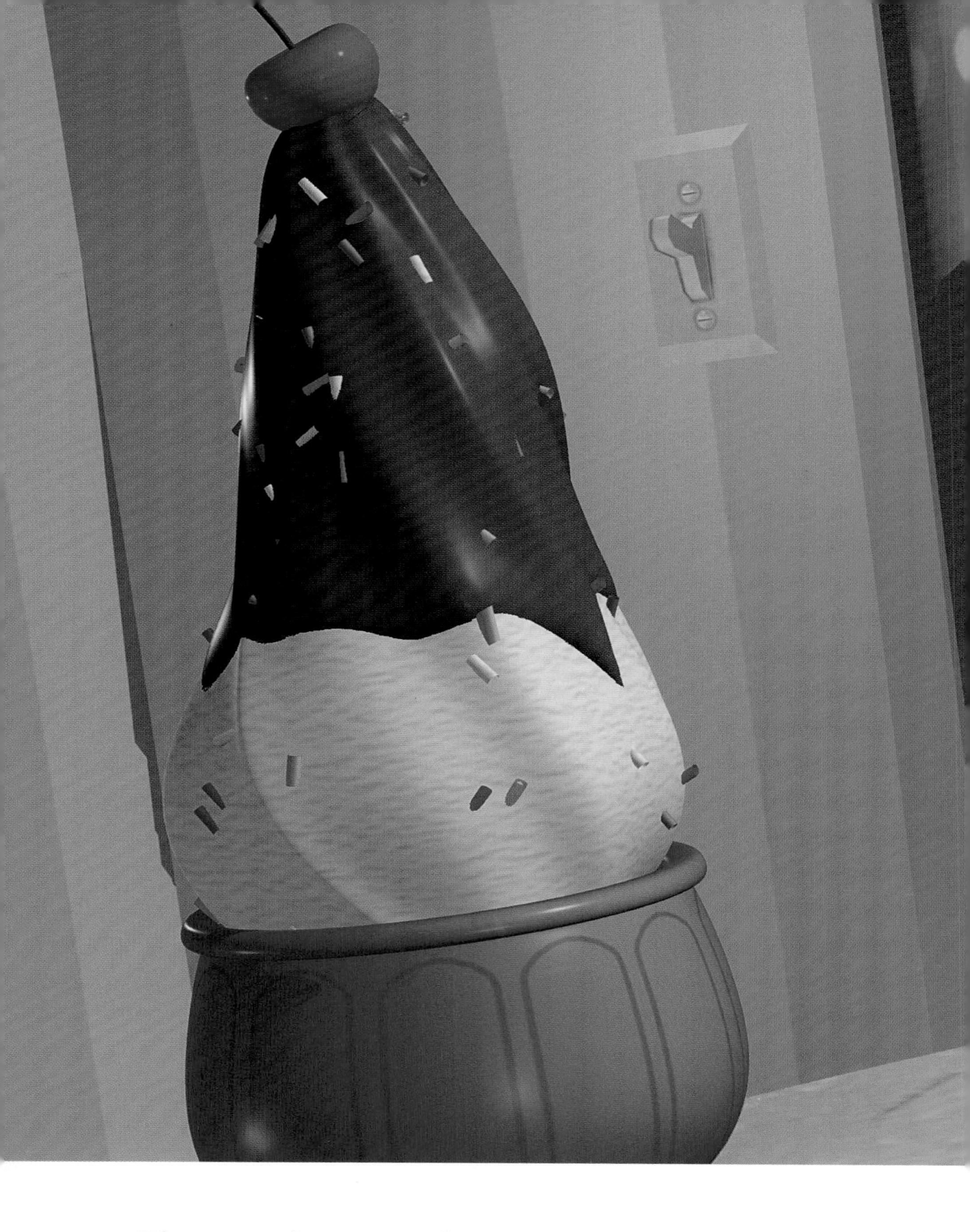

The magic turned mom and dad
into ice cream sundaes!

"What can we do?" asked Warren.

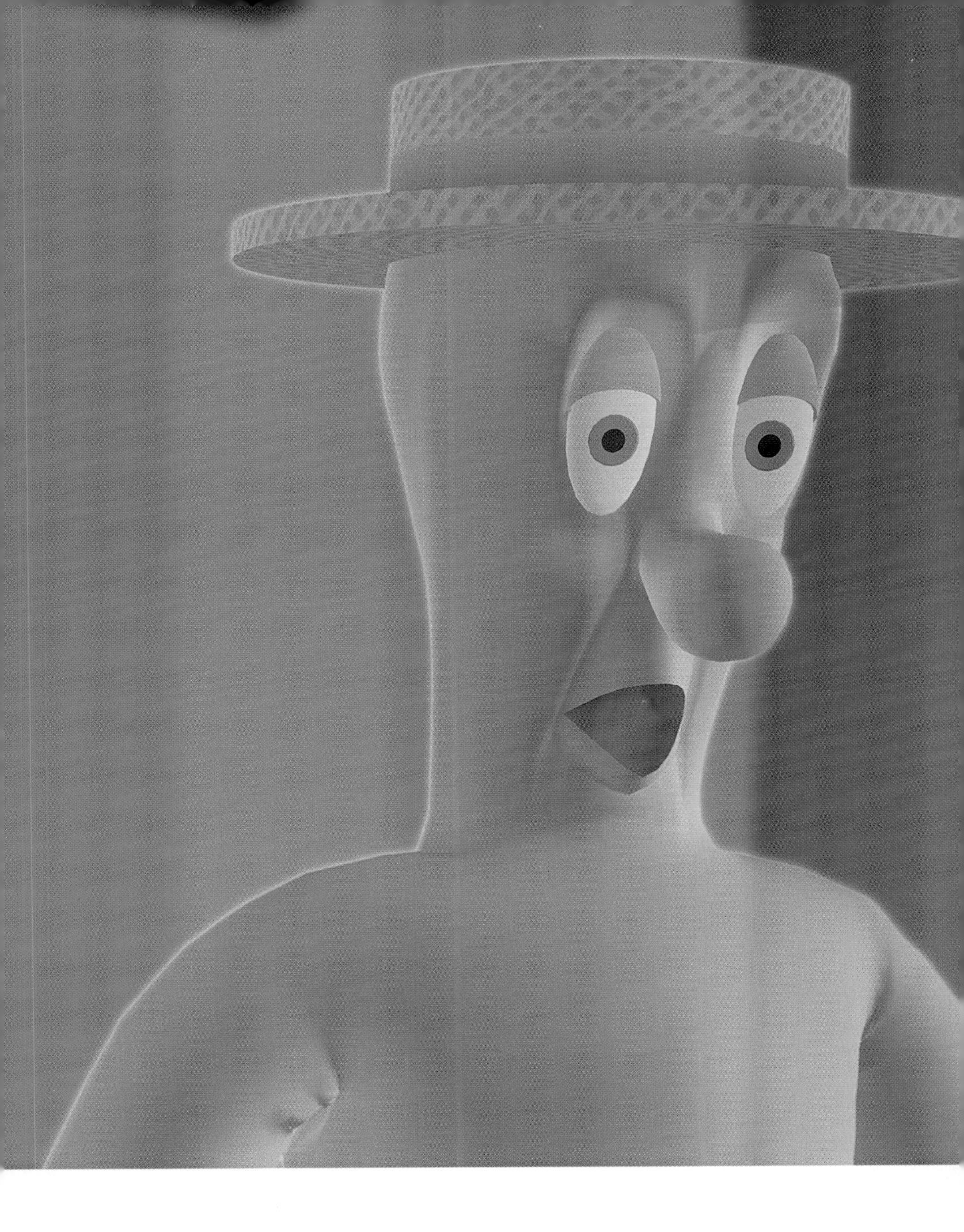

"This is bad!" said Johnny the Ghost.

"I will fix it!" Tracy told them.

She read a new spell.

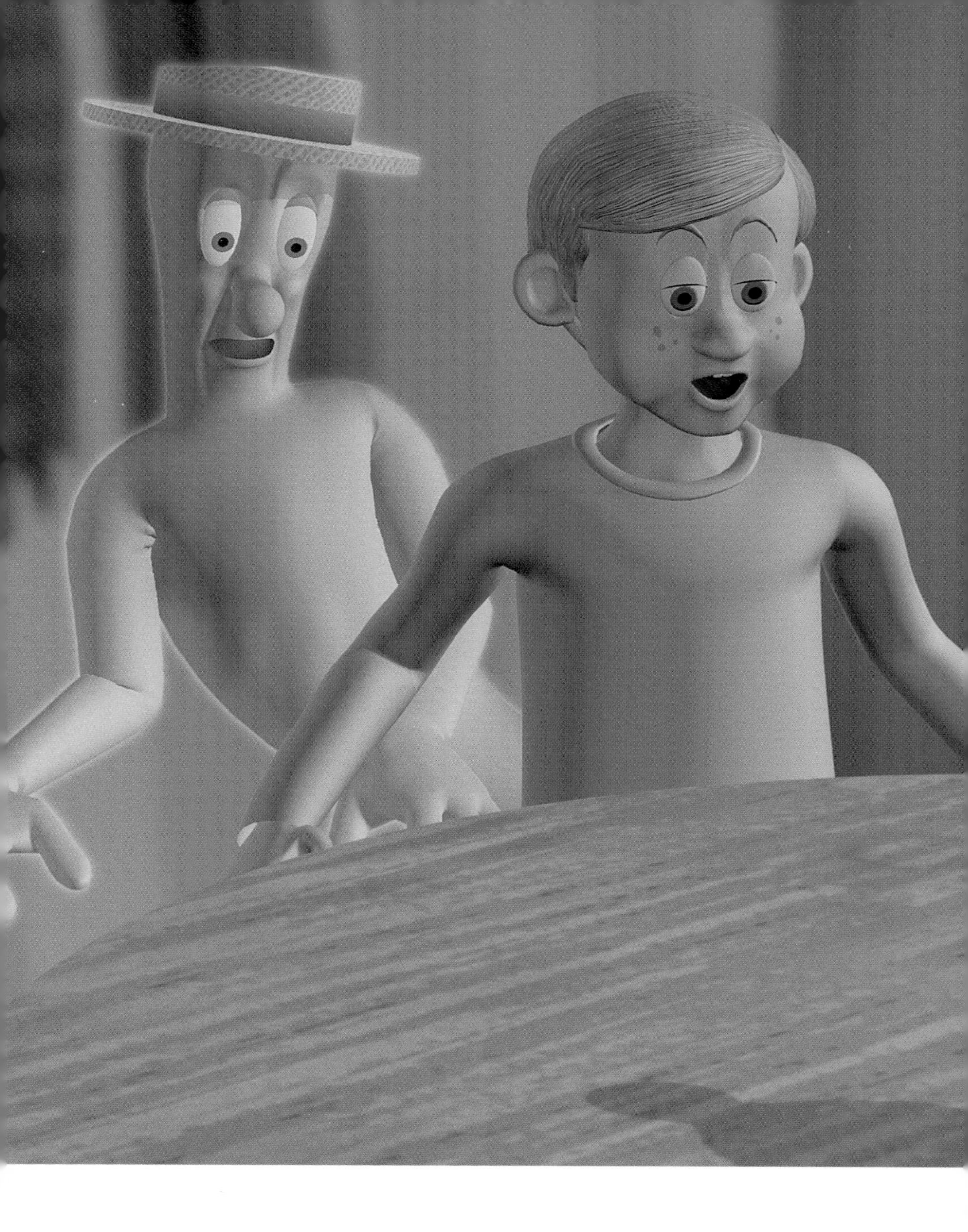

The new spell made the ice cream sundaes dance!

"Your mom and dad are good dancers!" said Johnny.

"We have to change them back!" Warren cried.

Johnny put the sundaes in the fridge.
Then he played some cool music!

"I hope they like my songs,"
Johnny said.

Tracy needed some new magic.

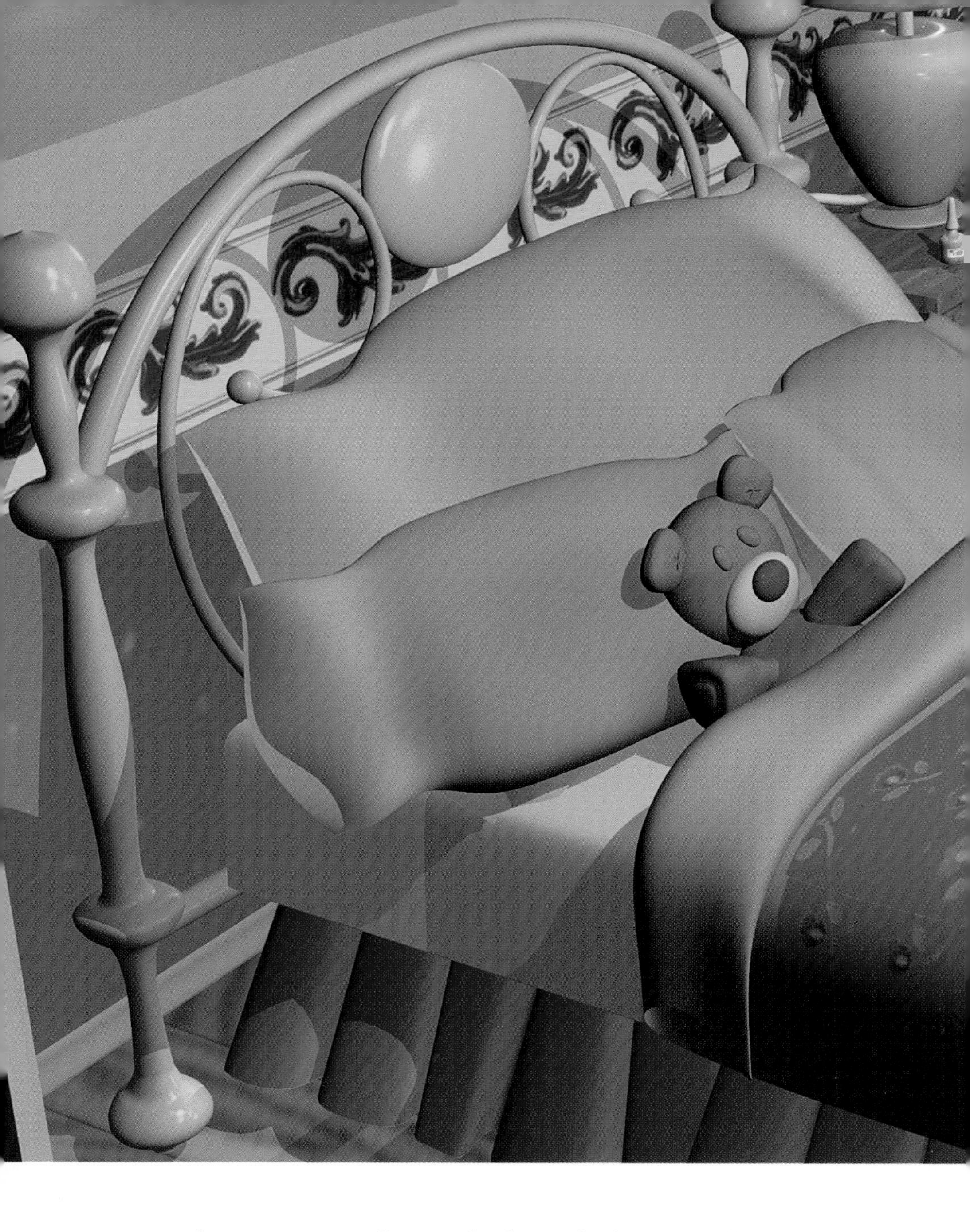

At last Tracy found the right spell!

Zap! The new spell hit the
ice cream sundaes.

Mom and dad were back!

"I felt a bit cold," Dad said.

"Me too," Mom said.

Tracy and Warren gave them a big hug.

Note to parents and teachers about Monster By Mistake Readers:

We trust your young readers will enjoy developing their reading skills with these great stories. Here is a simple guide to help you choose the right level for your child:

Level One Monster Readers

These stories are carefully written to build the confidence of beginning readers. They have been written to North American curriculum standards for Grade 1.

Featuring:

- short, simple sentences
- easy-to-recognize words
- exciting images to support the story

Level Two Monster Readers

Designed to build confidence of a new reader. They have been written to North American curriculum standards for Grade 2.

Featuring:

- slightly more difficult vocabulary
- more complex sentence and story structures
- exciting images to support the story

Level Three: Chapter books

Designed to appeal to both the advanced reader and the reluctant reader. They have been written to North American curriculum standards for Grades 3 and 4.

Featuring:

- complete plots based on the television episode
- controlled vocabulary and general readability
- stories deal with real life issues such as bullying, self-esteem and problem solving

Our Educational Consultant, Paul Kropp, is an author, editor and educator. His work includes young adult novels, novels for reluctant readers and the bestselling resource *How to Make Your Child a Reader for Life.*
Visit his website: www.paulkropp.com

Monster By Mistake Series is produced by CCI Entertainment Ltd. and Catapult Productions
Series Executive Producers: Arnie Zipursky and Kim Davidson
Based on the Screenplay "Just Desserts" by Lawrence S. Mirkin

Text Design: Counterpunch
Cover Design: Darrin La Framboise

1 2 3 4 5 6 07 06 05 04 03 02

Printed and bound in Canada

Contact Stewart House Publishing at info@stewarthousepub.com or 1-866-474-3478

National Library of Canada Cataloguing in Publication

Mayerson, Mark
Just desserts / created by Mark Mayerson; adapted by Paul Kropp.

(Monster by mistake)
Based on an episode of the television program, Monster by mistake.
Level 1.
For use in Kindergarten to grade 1.
ISBN 1-55366-320-9

I. Kropp, Paul, 1948– II. Catapult (Firm), III. Title. IV. Series.

PS8576.A8685J88 2002 jC813'.6 C2002-903657-7
PZ7